The Lady Or The Tiger?

and
The Discourager of Hesitancy

by

Frank R. Stockton

Compl

D0830654

First printing by Worthington Press 1995

Worthington Press,
a division of PAGES, Inc.
801 94th Avenue North, St. Petersburg, Florida 33702

Printed in the United States of America

2 4 6 8 10 9 7 5 3 1

ISBN 0-87406-798-7

The Lady or the Tiger?

IN the very olden time there lived a semi-barbaric king, whose ideas, though somewhat polished and sharpened by the progressiveness of distant Latin neighbors, were still large, florid, and untrammeled, as became the half of him which was barbaric. He was a man of exuberant fancy, and, withal, of an authority so irresistible that, at his will, he turned his varied fancies into facts. He was greatly given to self-communing; and when he and himself agreed upon anything, the thing was done. When every member of his domestic and political systems moved smoothly in its appointed course, his nature was bland and genial; but whenever there was a little hitch, and some of his orbs got out of their orbits, he was blander and more genial still, for nothing pleased him so much as to make the crooked straight, and crush down uneven places. Among the borrowed notions by which his barbarism had become semified was that of the public arena, in which, by exhibitions of manly and beastly valor, the minds of his subjects were refined and cultured.

But even here the exuberant and barbaric fancy asserted itself. The arena of the king was built not to give the people an opportunity of hearing the rhapsodies of dying gladiators, nor to enable them to view the inevitable conclusion of a conflict between religious opinions and hungry jaws, but for purposes far better adapted to widen and develop the mental energies of the people. This vast amphitheatre, with its encircling galleries, its mysterious vaults, and its unseen passages, was an agent of poetic justice, in which crime was punished, or virtue rewarded, by the decrees of an impartial and incorruptible chance. When a subject was accused of a crime of sufficient importance to interest the king, public notice was given that on an appointed day the fate of the accused person would be decided in the king's arena—a structure which well deserved its name for, although its form and plan were borrowed from afar, its purpose emanated solely from the brain of this man, who, every barleycorn a king, knew no tradition to which he owed more allegiance than pleased his fancy, and who ingrafted on every adopted form of human thought and action the rich growth of his barbaric idealism. When all the people had assembled in the galleries, and the king, surrounded by his court, sat high up on his throne of royal state on one side of the arena, he gave a signal, a door beneath him opened, and the accused subject stepped out into the amphitheatre. Directly opposite him, on the other side of the enclosed space, were two doors, exactly alike and side by side. It was the duty and the privilege of the person on trial to walk directly to these doors and open one of them. He could open either door he pleased: he was subject to no guidance or influence but that of the aforementioned impartial and incorruptible chance. If he opened the one, there came out of it a hungry tiger, the fiercest and most cruel that could be procured, which immediately sprang upon him and tore him to pieces, as a punishment for his guilt. The moment that the case of the criminal was thus decided, doleful iron bells were clanged, great wails went up from the hired mourners posted on the outer rim of the arena, and the vast audience, with bowed heads and downcast hearts, wended slowly their homeward way, mourning greatly that one so young and fair, or so old and respected, should have merited so dire a fate.

But if the accused person opened the other door, there came forth from it a lady, the most suitable to his years and station that his Majesty could select among his fair subjects; and to this lady he was immediately married, as a reward of his innocence. It mattered not that he might already possess a wife and family, or that his affections might be engaged upon an object of his own selection: the king allowed no such subordinate arrangements to interfere with his great scheme of retribution and reward. The exercises, as in the other instance, took place immediately, and in the arena. Another door opened beneath the king, and a priest, followed by a band of choristers, and dancing maidens blowing joyous airs on golden horns and treading an epithalamic measure, advanced to where the pair stood side by side; and the wedding was promptly and cheerily solemnized. Then the gay brass bells rang forth their merry peals, the people shouted glad hurrahs, and the innocent man, preceded by children strewing flowers on his path, led his bride to his home.

This was the king's semibarbaric method of administering justice. Its perfect fairness is obvious. The criminal could not know out of which door would come the lady: he opened either he pleased, without having the slightest idea whether, in the next instant, he was to be devoured or married. On some occasions the tiger came out of one door, and on some out of the other. The decisions of this tribunal were not only fair, they were positively determinate: the accused person was instantly punished if he found himself guilty; and if innocent, he was rewarded on the spot, whether he liked it or not. There was no escape from the judgments of the king's arena.

The institution was a very popular one. When the people gathered together on one of the great trial days, they never knew whether they were to witness a bloody slaughter or a hilarious wedding. This element of uncertainty lent an interest to the occasion which it could not otherwise have attained. Thus the masses were entertained and pleased, and the thinking part of the community could bring no charge of unfairness against this plan; for did not the accused person have the whole matter in his own hands?

This semibarbaric king had a daughter as blooming as his most florid fancies, and with a soul as fervent and imperious as his own. As is usual in such cases, she was the apple of his eye, and was loved by him above all humanity. Among his courtiers was a young man of that fineness of blood and lowness of station common to the conventional heroes of romance who love royal maidens. This royal maiden was well satisfied with her lover, for he was handsome and brave to a degree unsurpassed in all this kingdom; and she loved him with an ardor that had enough of barbarism in it to make it exceedingly warm and strong. This love-affair moved on happily for many months, until one day the king happened to discover its existence. He did not hesitate nor waver in regard to his duty in the premises. The youth was immediately cast into prison, and a day was appointed for his trial in the king's arena. This, of course, was an especially important occasion; and his Majesty, as well as all the people, were greatly interested in the workings and development of this trial. Never before had such a case occurred; never before had a subject dared to love the daughter of a king. In afteryears such things became commonplace enough; but then they were, in no slight degree, novel and startling.

The tiger-cages of the kingdom were searched for the most savage and relentless beasts, from which the fiercest monster might be selected for the arena; and the ranks of maiden youth and beauty throughout the land were carefully surveyed by competent judges, in order that the young man might have a fitting bride in case fate did not determine for him a different destiny. Of course everybody knew that the deed with which the accused was charged had been done. He had loved the princess, and neither he, she, nor any one else thought of denying the fact; but the king would not think of allowing any fact of this kind to interfere with the workings of the tribunal, in which he took such great delight and satisfaction. No matter how the affair turned out, the youth would be disposed of; and the king would take an aesthetic pleasure in watching the course of events, which would determine whether or not the young man had done wrong in allowing himself to love the princess.

The appointed day arrived. From far and near the people gathered, and thronged the great galleries of the arena; and crowds, unable to gain admittance, massed themselves against its outside walls. The king and his court were in their places, opposite the twin doors—those fateful portals, so terrible in their similarity.

All was ready. The signal was given. A door beneath the royal party opened, and the lover of the princess walked into the arena. Tall, beautiful, fair, his appearance was greeted with a low hum of admiration and anxiety. Half the audience had not known so grand a youth had lived among them. No wonder the princess loved him! What a terrible thing for him to be there!

As the youth advanced into the arena, he turned, as the custom was, to bow to the king: but he did not think at all of that royal personage; his eyes were fixed upon the princess, who sat to the right of her father. Had it not been for the moiety of barbarism in her nature it is probable that lady would not have been there; but her intense and fervid soul would not allow her to be absent on an occasion in which she was so terribly interested. From the moment that the decree had gone forth that her lover should decide his fate in the king's arena, she had thought of nothing, night or day, but this great event and the various subjects connected with it. Possessed of more power, influence, and force of character than any one who had ever before been interested in such a case, she had done what no other person had done—she had possessed herself of the secret of the doors. She knew in which of the two rooms that lay behind those doors stood the cage of the tiger, with its open front, and in which waited the lady. Through these thick doors, heavily curtained with skins on the inside, it was impossible that any noise or suggestion should come from within to the person who should approach to raise the latch of one of them; but gold, and the power of a woman's will, had brought the secret to the princess.

And not only did she know in which room stood the lady ready to emerge, all blushing and radiant, should her door be opened, but she knew who the lady was. It was one of the fairest and loveliest of the damsels of the court who had been selected as the reward of the accused youth, should he be proved innocent of the crime of aspiring to one so far above him; and the princess hated her. Often had she seen, or imagined that she had seen, this fair creature throwing glances of admiration upon the person of her lover, and some-times she thought these glances were per-ceived and even returned. Now and then she had seen them talking together; it was but for a moment or two, but much can be said in a brief space; it may have been on most unimportant topics, but how could she know that? The girl was lovely, but she had dared to raise her eyes to the loved one of the princess; and, with all the intensity of the savage blood transmitted to her through long lines of wholly barbaric ancestors, she hated the woman who blushed and trembled behind that silent door.

When her lover turned and looked at her, and his eye met hers as she sat there paler and whiter than any one in the vast ocean of anxious faces about her, he saw, by that power of quick perception which is given to those whose souls are one, that she knew behind which door crouched the tiger, and behind which stood the lady. He had expected her to know it. He understood her nature, and his soul was assured that she would never rest until she had made plain to herself this thing, hidden to all other lookers-on, even to the king. The only hope for the youth in which there was any element of certainty was based upon the success of the princess in discovering this mystery; and the moment he looked upon her, he saw she had succeeded, as in his soul he knew she would succeed.

Then it was that his quick and anxious glance asked the question, "Which?" It was as plain to her as if he shouted it from where he stood. There was not an instant to be lost. The question was asked in a flash; it must be answered in another.

Her right arm lay on the cushioned parapet before her. She raised her hand, and made a slight, quick movement toward the right. No one but her lover saw her. Every eye but his was fixed on the man in the arena.

He turned, and with a firm and rapid step he walked across the empty space.

Every heart stopped beating, every breath was held, every eye was fixed immovably upon that man. Without the slightest hesitation, he went to the door on the right, and opened it.

Now, the point of the story is this: Did the tiger come out of that door, or did the lady?

The more we reflect upon this question the harder it is to answer. It involves a study of the human heart which leads us through devious mazes of passion, out of which it is difficult to find our way. Think of it, fair reader, not as if the decision of the question depended upon yourself, but upon that hot-blooded, semibarbaric princess, her soul at a white heat beneath the combined fires of despair and jealousy. She had lost him, but who should have him?

How often, in her waking hours and in her dreams, had she started in wild horror and covered her face with her hands as she thought of her lover opening the door on the other side of which waited the cruel fangs of the tiger!

But how much oftener had she seen him at the other door! How in her grievous reveries had she gnashed her teeth and torn her hair when she saw his start of rapturous delight as he opened the door of the lady! How her soul had burned in agony when she had seen him rush to meet that woman, with her flushing cheek and sparkling eye of triumph; when she had seen him lead her forth, his whole frame kindled with the joy of recovered life; when she had heard the glad shouts from the multitude, and the wild ringing of the happy bells; when she had seen the priest, with his joyous followers, advance to the couple, and make them man and wife before her very eyes; and when she had seen them walk away together upon their path of flowers, followed by the tremendous shouts of the hilarious multitude, in which her one despairing shriek was lost and drowned!

Would it not be better for him to die at once, and go to wait for her in the blessed regions of semibarbaric futurity?

And yet, that awful tiger, those shrieks, that blood!

Her decision had been indicated in an instant, but it had been made after days and nights of anguished deliberation. She had known she would be asked, she had decided what she would answer, and, without the slightest hesitation, she had moved her hand to the right.

The question of her decision is one not to be lightly considered, and it is not for me to presume to set myself up as the one person able to answer it. And so I leave it with all of you: Which came out of the opened door—the lady or the tiger?

The Discourager
of Hesitancy

A Continuation of
"The Lady or the Tiger?"

The Discourager of Hesitancy

IT was nearly a year after the occurrence of that event in the arena of the semibarbaric king, known as the incident of the lady or the tiger, that there came to the palace of this monarch a deputation of five strangers from a far country. These men, of venerable and dignified aspect and demeanor, were received by a high officer of the court, and to him they made known their errand.

"Most noble officer," said the speaker of the deputation, "it so happened that one of our countrymen was present here, in your capital city, on that momentous occasion when a young man who had dared to aspire to the hand of your king's daughter had been placed in the arena, in the midst of the assembled multitude, and ordered to open one of two doors, not knowing whether a ferocious tiger would spring out upon him, or a beauteous lady would advance, ready to become his bride. Our fellow-citizen who was then present was a man of supersensitive feelings, and at the moment when the youth was about to open the door he was so fearful lest he should behold a horrible spectacle that his nerves failed him, and he fled precipitately from the arena, and, mounting his camel, rode homeward as fast as he could go.

"We were all very much interested in the story which our countryman told us, and we were extremely sorry that he did not wait to see the end of the affair. We hoped, however, that in a few weeks some traveller from your city would come among us and bring us further news, but up to the day when we left our country no such traveller had arrived. At last it was determined that the only thing to be done was to send a deputation to this country, and to ask the question: 'Which came out of the open door, the lady or the tiger?'"

When the high officer had heard the mission of this most respectable deputation, he led the five strangers into an inner room, where they were seated upon soft cushions, and where he ordered coffee, pipes, sherbet, and other semibarbaric refreshments to be served to them. Then, taking his seat before them, he thus addressed the visitors:

"Most noble strangers, before answering the question you have come so far to ask, I will relate to you an incident which occurred not very long after that to which you have referred. It is well known in all regions hereabout that our great king is very fond of the presence of beautiful women about his court. All the ladies in waiting upon the queen and royal family are most lovely maidens, brought here from every part of the kingdom. The fame of this concourse of beauty, unequalled in any other royal court, has spread far and wide, and had it not been for the equally widespread fame of the systems of impetuous justice adopted by our king, many foreigners would doubtless have visited our court.

"But not very long ago there arrived here from a distant land a prince of distinguished appearance and undoubted rank. To such a one, of course, a royal audience was granted, and our king met him very graciously, and begged him to make known the object of his visit. Thereupon the prince informed his Royal Highness that, having heard of the superior beauty of the ladies of his court, he had come to ask permission to make one of them his wife.

"When our king heard this bold announcement, his face reddened, he turned uneasily on his throne, and we were all in dread lest some quick words of furious condemnation should leap from out his quivering lips. But by a mighty effort he controlled himself, and after a moment's silence he turned to the prince and said: 'Your request is granted. Tomorrow at noon you shall wed one of the fairest damsels of our court.' Then turning to his officers, he said: 'Give orders that everything be prepared for a wedding in this palace at high noon tomorrow. Convey this royal prince to suitable apartments. Send to him tailors, bootmakers, hatters, jewelers, armorers, men of every craft whose services he may need. Whatever he asks, provide. And let all be ready for the ceremony tomorrow.'

"'But, your Majesty,' exclaimed the prince, 'before we make these preparations, I would like—'

"'Say no more!' roared the king. 'My royal orders have been given, and nothing more is needed to be said. You asked a boon. I granted it, and I will hear no more on the subject. Farewell, my prince, until tomorrow noon.'

"At this the king arose and left the audience chamber, while the prince was hurried away to the apartments selected for him. Here came to him tailors, hatters, jewelers, and every one who was needed to fit him out in grand attire for the wedding. But the mind of the prince was much troubled and perplexed.

"'I do not understand,' he said to his attendants, 'this precipitancy of action. When am I to see the ladies, that I may choose among them? I wish opportunity, not only to gaze upon their forms and faces, but to become acquainted with their relative intellectual development.'

"'We can tell you nothing,' was the answer. 'What our king thinks right, that will he do. More than this we know not.'

"'His Majesty's notions seem to be very peculiar,' said the prince, 'and, so far as I can see, they do not at all agree with mine.'

"At that moment an attendant whom the prince had not before noticed came and stood beside him. This was a broad-shouldered man of cheery aspect, who carried, its hilt in his right hand, and its broad back resting on his broad arm, an enormous cimeter, the upturned edge of which was keen and bright as any razor. Holding this formidable weapon as tenderly as though it had been a sleeping infant, this man drew closer to the prince and bowed.

"'Who are you?' exclaimed his Highness, starting back at the sight of the frightful weapon.

"'I,' said the other, with a courteous smile, 'am the Discourager of Hesitancy. When our king makes known his wishes to any one, a subject or visitor, whose disposition in some little points may be supposed not wholly to coincide with that of his Majesty, I am appointed to attend him closely, that, should he think of pausing in the path of obedience to the royal will, he may look at me, and proceed.'

"The prince looked at him, and proceeded to be measured for a coat.

"The tailors and shoemakers and hatters worked all night, and the next morning, when everything was ready, and the hour of noon was drawing nigh, the prince again anxiously inquired of his attendants when he might expect to be introduced to the ladies.

"'The king will attend to that,' they said. 'We know nothing of the matter.'

"'Your Highness,' said the Discourager of Hesitancy, approaching with a courtly bow, 'will observe the excellent quality of this edge.' And drawing a hair from his head, he dropped it upon the upturned edge of his cimeter, upon which it was cut in two at the moment of touching.

"The prince glanced, and turned upon his heel.

"Now came officers to conduct him to the grand hall of the palace, in which the ceremony was to be performed. Here the prince found the king seated on the throne, with his nobles, his courtiers, and his officers standing about him in magnificent array. The prince was led to a position in front of the king, to whom he made obeisance, and then said:

"'Your Majesty, before I proceed further—'

"At this moment an attendant, who had approached with a long scarf of delicate silk, wound it about the lower part of the prince's face so quickly and adroitly that he was obliged to cease speaking. Then, with wonderful dexterity, the rest of the scarf was wound around the prince's head, so that he was completely blindfolded. Thereupon the attendant quickly made openings in the scarf over the mouth and ears, so that the prince might breathe and hear, and fastening the ends of the scarf securely, he retired.

"The first impulse of the prince was to

snatch the silken folds from his head and face, but, as he raised his hands to do so, he heard beside him the voice of the Discourager of Hesitancy, who gently whispered: 'I am here, your Highness.' And, with a shudder, the arms of the prince fell down by his side.

"Now before him he heard the voice of a priest, who had begun the marriage service in use in that semibarbaric country. At his side he could hear a delicate rustle, which seemed to proceed from fabrics of soft silk. Gently putting forth his hand, he felt folds of such silk close beside him. Then came the voice of the priest requesting him to take the hand of the lady by his side; and reaching forth his right hand, the prince received within it another hand, so small, so soft, so delicately fashioned, and so delightful to the touch, that a thrill went through his being. Then, as was the custom of the country, the priest first asked the lady would she have this man to be her husband; to which the answer gently came, in the sweetest voice he had ever heard: 'I will.'

"Then ran raptures rampant through the prince's blood. The touch, the tone, enchanted him. All the ladies of that court were beautiful, the Discourager was behind him, and through his parted scarf he boldly answered: 'Yes, I will.'

"Whereupon the priest pronounced them man and wife.

"Now the prince heard a little bustle about him, the long scarf was rapidly unrolled from his head, and he turned, with a start, to gaze upon his bride. To his utter amazement, there was no one there. He stood alone. Unable on the instant to ask a question or say a word, he gazed blankly about him.

"Then the king arose from his throne, and came down, and took him by the hand.

" 'Where is my wife?' gasped the prince.

"'She is here,' said the king, leading him to a curtained doorway at the side of the hall.

"The curtains were drawn aside, and the prince, entering, found himself in a long apartment, near the opposite wall of which stood a line of forty ladies, all dressed in rich attire, and each one apparently more beautiful than the rest.

"Waving his hand toward the line, the king said to the prince: 'There is your bride! Approach, and lead her forth! But remember this: that if you attempt to take away one of the unmarried damsels of our court, your execution shall be instantaneous. Now, delay no longer. Step up and take your bride.'

"The prince, as in a dream, walked slowly along the line of ladies, and then walked slowly back again. Nothing could he see about any one of them to indicate that she was more of a bride than the others. Their dresses were all similar, they all blushed, they all looked up and then looked down. They all had charming little hands. Not one spoke a word. Not one lifted a finger to make a sign. It was evident that the orders given them had been very strict.

"'Why this delay?' roared the king. 'If I had been married this day to one so fair as the lady who wedded you, I should not wait one second to claim her.'

"The bewildered prince walked again up and down the line. And this time there was a slight change in the countenances of two of the ladies. One of the fairest gently smiled as he passed her. Another, just as beautiful, slightly frowned.

"'Now,' said the prince to himself, 'I am sure that it is one of those two ladies whom I have married. But which? One smiled. And would not any woman smile when she saw, in such a case, her husband coming toward her? Then again, on the other hand, would not any woman frown when she saw her husband come toward her and fail to claim her? Would she not knit her lovely brows? Would she not inwardly say, "It is I! Don't you know it? Don't you feel it? Come!" But if this woman had not been married, would she not frown when she saw the man looking at her? Would she not say inwardly, "Don't stop at me! It is the next but one. It is two ladies above. Go on!" Then again, the one who married me did not see my face. Would she not now smile if she thought me comely? But if I wedded the one who frowned, could she restrain her disapprobation if she did not like me? Smiles invite the approach of true love. A frown is a reproach to a tardy advance. A smile—'

"'Now, hear me!' loudly cried the king. 'In ten seconds, if you do not take the lady we have given you, she who has just been made your bride shall be your widow.'

"And, as the last word was uttered, the Discourager of Hesitancy stepped close behind the prince and whispered: 'I am here!'

"Now the prince could not hesitate an instant; he stepped forward and took one of the two ladies by the hand.

"Loud rang the bells, loud cheered the people, and the king came forward to congratulate the prince. He had taken his lawful bride.

"Now, then," said the high officer to the deputation of five strangers from a far country, "when you can decide among yourselves which lady the prince chose, the one who smiled or the one who frowned, then will I tell you which came out of the open door, the lady or the tiger!"

At the latest accounts the five strangers had not yet decided.

About the Author

Frank Richard Stockton was born on April 5, 1834, in Philadelphia, Pennsylvania. Bothered with health problems all his life, Stockton found joy in telling stories. He was also an artist and made a good living by drawing illustrations. Eventually, he focused on writing, mainly fairy tales and other children's stories.

Stockton's most famous story, "The Lady or the Tiger?", earned him immediate respect and admiration. The question of "the lady or the tiger?" has been debated by readers ever since.

Frank Stockton died in 1902.